Library of Congress Cataloging in Publication Data

Walt Disney Productions presents Button soup. (Disney's wonderful world of reading, #28) Daisy tricks her stingy Uncle Scrooge into making enough soup for the whole town—using just one button. I. Disney (Walt) Productions. II. Title: Button soup. PZ7.W16897 [E] 74-28376 ISBN 0-394-82562-4 ISBN 0-394-92562-9 (lib. bdg.)

Manufactured in the United States of America

3 4 5 6

GROLIER
BOOK CLUB EDITION

G H I J K

R

A long time ago a traveler named Daisy
was riding the stagecoach out West.
She was going to visit her old Uncle Scrooge.
Daisy was tired and thirsty and very hungry.
She could hardly wait to reach her uncle's house.

When the stagecoach pulled into town,
everyone came out to see who was on it.

Goofy the Sheriff walked up to Daisy.

"Howdy," he said. "What can I do for you?"

"I'm looking for Scrooge McDuck," said Daisy.

"Scrooge McDuck!" cried Goofy the Sheriff.
"If you are as tired and hungry as you look,
you should go to the hotel!"

Then he pointed to a little yellow house.

"Old Scrooge lives there," he said.
"But no one ever pays him a visit."

"That is right," said Miss Clarabelle.
"Old Scrooge must be the stingiest fellow
in the whole West!"

"Yup," said Goofy. "He's the stingiest fellow in the West, all right."

"I have met stingy fellows before," said Daisy. "Maybe I can teach my uncle a lesson."

So Daisy went straight to the yellow house
and knocked on the door.

When Uncle Scrooge opened the door,
Daisy threw her arms around his neck.

"Surprise!" she cried. "I have come to pay
a visit, Uncle."

Scrooge did not look happy to see his niece.

"I did not ask you to come!" he shouted.

But Daisy did not listen to him.
She walked into the house.
"I am very hungry, Uncle," she said.
"What do you have to eat?"

"You won't find any food here," said Scrooge.
He tried to hide some dirty dishes.
"There is no food in the house!" he cried.

"Poor Uncle," said Daisy. "You must be starved!"
And she went to the cupboard and took out
a big black pot.

There on a shelf was a basket of fried chicken.

"Aha," she thought. "My uncle is not as poor
as he pretends to be."

Daisy began to fill the pot with water.
Uncle Scrooge jumped up and down.
"You cannot cook here!" he said.
"I just told you I have no food!"

But Daisy did not listen to him.
She lit a fire under the pot.
"I don't need any food," she said.
Her uncle's mouth fell open.
"What in the world can you cook
without food?" he asked.

Daisy took out an old red button.

She held it under her uncle's nose and rolled it slowly between her fingers.

"With just this button," she said, "I can cook enough soup to fill that pot."

"You can make soup
with just one button?"
said Scrooge. "I don't
believe it!"

He watched Daisy
drop the red button
into the pot.

"What do you
call it?" asked
Uncle Scrooge.

"Button soup,"
said Daisy.

Uncle Scrooge
watched Daisy
sniff the soup.
"H-m-m-m-m,"
she thought.
"The stingiest fellow
in the West is getting
curious!"

Now Uncle Scrooge
sniffed the soup.
He did not smell
a thing.

Daisy began to stir very quickly.
As she stirred, she said,
"Whenever I make this soup at home,
I always use some salt and pepper.
But since you have no food in the house,
I guess you have no salt and pepper."

"I don't have any food," said Scrooge.
"But I always save some salt and pepper
for a rainy day."

He lit a candle, opened a door in the ceiling, and climbed up to the attic.

The attic walls were covered with jars of spice.
Scrooge held his candle up to see them better.
He picked out jars of salt and pepper to add
to the button soup.

Daisy poured the salt and pepper
into the pot.

Uncle Scrooge watched.

He could hardly wait
to taste the button soup.

Daisy began to stir again.

As she stirred, she said:
"I once made this soup
with an old soup bone.
It really was delicious.
But if you have no
food, one button
will have to do."

"If all you need is an old soup bone,"
said Scrooge, "I might be able to find one."
He took a lantern and ran down to the cellar.

Scrooge's cellar looked just like a butcher shop.
He had hams and chickens and turkeys and beef.
He picked out a juicy bone to add to the button sou

When Scrooge came back with the bone,
Daisy dropped it into the pot.

The soup began to bubble and boil.

"It smells good!" said Scrooge.

"This soup won a blue ribbon at the State Fair,"
said Daisy. "But that time I used potatoes and
carrots."

"If the blue-ribbon soup
had potatoes and carrots,
we shall have them, too,"
said her uncle.

And he ran out
to the barn.

Up in the hayloft Scrooge had vegetables—
potatoes and carrots and big heads of cabbage.
He grabbed a pitchfork and tossed the hay.
He found some potatoes and carrots to add
to the button soup.

By this time the soup smelled so good
Uncle Scrooge was dying to taste it.

And every time Daisy named something
that would make the soup even better,
Uncle Scrooge rushed off to find it.

He ran to the woodshed
for onions and celery.

He milked the cow
to get Daisy some cream.

He dug up his garden
to get her some turnips.

And he carried everything
to the big black pot.

At last the button soup was ready to taste.
"This is too much soup for me," said Daisy.
"And this is too much soup for you. Let's ask
someone to share it with us!"

"Share it?" cried Scrooge. "Let's pour it into jars and save it. Food is hard to get."

"But Uncle Scrooge," said Daisy. "Don't you remember? We made THIS soup with just one button!"

"That's right!" said Scrooge. "So we did!"

So Daisy ran to everyone in town.

She ran to Goofy
the Sheriff.

She ran to the
ice cream parlor
to get Miss Clarabelle.

She ran to the general store for Mistress Minnie.

She ran to the barber shop for Mickey and Cowboy Donald.

And she told them all to come to Scrooge McDuck's house.

When they came in
Scrooge gave them each
a bowl.

"You sure are clever," said Miss Clarabelle.
"Scrooge is not the stingiest fellow in the West
any more!"

Daisy only winked her eye.

Soon they all sat down to a button soup feast.
And it really WAS delicious.

"What a clever niece I have," said Scrooge.
"She made this soup with JUST ONE BUTTON!"

When the time came for Daisy to leave,
Scrooge went to the stagecoach to see her off.
"Come back to visit me soon, Daisy," he said.

"After all," thought Scrooge, "such clever nieces don't grow on every bush!"